Walt Disney's
Mickey Mouse
The KITTEN-SITTERS

A GOLDEN BOOK, NEW YORK
Western Publishing Company, Inc.
Racine, Wisconsin 53404

Copyright © 1976 Walt Disney Productions. World rights reserved. Printed in the U.S.A.
No part of this book may be reproduced or copied in any form without written permission
from the copyright owner. GOLDEN®, GOLDEN & DESIGN®, A LITTLE GOLDEN
BOOK®, and A GOLDEN BOOK® are trademarks of Western Publishing Company, Inc.
ISBN 0-307-02038-X   S T

"Guess what!" said Mickey Mouse to his nephews, Morty and Ferdie. "We're going to be kitten-sitters. Minnie is going to leave Figaro the kitten with us tonight while she visits her Cousin Millie."

At that moment, there was a wild clucking and flapping and crowing from next door. Pluto the pup came racing across the lawn, with a big, angry rooster close behind him.

Pluto hid under the porch while Mickey shooed the rooster back to his own yard.

"Pluto!" scolded Minnie. "Chasing chickens again! Aren't you ashamed?"

Pluto *was* a bit ashamed, but only because he had let the rooster bully him. Creeping out from under the porch, he wagged his tail and sheepishly tried to grin.

"I think it's a good thing Figaro is going to stay with
you," said Minnie to Mickey. "Figaro is a little gentle-
man. He can teach Pluto how to behave."

With that, Minnie handed her kitten to Mickey.
Then she got into her car and drove away.

Minnie was scarcely out of sight, when Figaro jumped out of Mickey's arms and scampered into the house. In the kitchen, he saw a pitcher of cream that Mickey had forgotten to put away.

One short jump up to a chair seat, followed by a second jump to the tabletop, brought Figaro right to the cream. The pitcher wobbled, then tipped over. Cream spilled and ran off the table and onto the floor.

Pluto growled a warning growl as Figaro lapped up
the cream.

"Take it easy, Pluto," said Mickey, wiping up the
spilled cream. "Figaro is our guest."

When Figaro heard that, he wrinkled his nose at
Pluto and stuck out his little pink tongue.

Then he romped through the ashes in the fireplace
and left sooty footprints on the carpet.

"Figaro's a very *messy* little guest," said Mickey's
nephew Morty as he got out the vacuum cleaner.

At dinner time, Pluto ate his dog food, the way a good dog should. But no matter how Mickey and the boys coaxed, Figaro wouldn't touch the special kitty food Minnie had left for him. He did, at last, nibble some imported sardines.

"He's a *fussy* little guest," said Ferdie.

At bedtime, Pluto curled up in his basket without any complaint.

Did Figaro curl up on the fine, soft cushion Minnie had brought for him? He did not!

Instead, he got into bed with Morty and nipped at his toes. Then he got into bed with Ferdie and tickled both his ears. Finally, he bounced off to the kitchen, and the house became very still.

"Uncle Mickey," called Morty, "did you remember to close the kitchen window?"

"Oh, no!" cried Mickey. He jumped out of bed and ran to the kitchen.

The kitchen window was open, and Figaro the kitten was nowhere to be seen!

Mickey and the boys went through the house. They looked under every chair and behind every door. "Figaro!" they called.

They went out into the yard. They looked under
every bush and behind every tree.

No Figaro.

"He's really run away," Mickey decided at last. Morty and Ferdie followed Mickey back to the house, where Mickey put his coat on over his pajamas. "You two stay here," he told the boys. "Pluto and I will find Figaro. Leave the porch light on for us."

Pluto didn't wag his tail, and he didn't even try to grin as he got out of his cozy basket. But off he went to help Mickey in the search.

They went to Minnie's house first, but Figaro hadn't gone home.

Then they went to the park down the street. "Have you seen a little black and white kitten?" Mickey asked the policeman at the gate.

"I certainly have!" answered the policeman. "He was by the pond, teasing the ducks!"

Mickey and Pluto hurried to the pond.

Figaro wasn't there. He had been there, though. He had left behind some small, muddy footprints and several large, excited ducks.

Mickey and Pluto followed the trail of footprints to Main Street, where they met a crew of firemen.

"I'm looking for a black and white kitten," said Mickey to the firemen.

"Is that so?" said one of the firemen. "We just res-

cued a black and white kitten. He had climbed a tele-
phone pole and couldn't get down again. He ran
through that alley."

In the alley, a dairy truck driver was busily cleaning
up broken eggs in his truck.

"Have you seen a kitten?" asked Mickey.

"Have I!" said the driver. "He jumped into my
truck and knocked over dozens of eggs!"

Mickey groaned as he paid for the smashed eggs.

When Mickey and Pluto finally trudged home, it was dawn. They had searched the whole town. They had even been to the police station, but they had not found Figaro.

"What will Aunt Minnie say?" asked the boys.

"I hate to think what Aunt Minnie will say," answered poor Mickey.

Before long, Minnie drove up. Mickey and the boys
looked worried as they went out to meet her.

"Where is Figaro?" asked Minnie.

No one answered.

"Something has happened to him!" Minnie was upset, and she was angry. "Can't I trust you to watch *just
one* sweet little kitten for me?"

Just then there was a loud clucking and squawking from the yard next door. At least a dozen frantic hens came flapping over the fence.

Close behind the hens came the big, angry rooster. Close behind the rooster came Figaro the kitten. Figaro's fur was rumpled, and he carried a long tail feather between his teeth.

"*There's* your sweet little kitten!" said Mickey.

"Figaro!" cried Minnie, not believing her eyes.

At the sound of her voice, Figaro skidded to a sudden stop. He sat down and mewed a gentle kitten mew. He tried quickly to smooth his dusty fur with his little pink tongue.

"He ran away last night," explained Mickey. "He teased the ducks in the park and broke the eggs in the dairy truck and—"

"And now he's chasing chickens!" finished Minnie.

"I hoped he'd teach Pluto some manners," Minnie
went on. "Instead, Pluto has been teaching him to do
those naughty things. Teasing ducks! Chasing chickens! The very idea! I'll *never* leave him here again."

"It wasn't Pluto's fault!" protested Morty.

"He didn't do anything bad," added Ferdie. "He stayed up all night, trying to find Figaro."

But Minnie wouldn't listen. She picked up Figaro, got into her car, and drove quickly away.

"Don't worry, boys," said Mickey. "We'll tell her the whole story later, when she's not so upset."

"Please don't tell her too soon," begged Morty. "As long as Aunt Minnie thinks Pluto is a naughty dog, we won't have to kitten-sit with Figaro."

Mickey smiled. "Maybe we *should* wait a little while. We could all use some peace and quiet.

"I did learn one thing," yawned Mickey as he stretched out beside Pluto under a shady tree. "There's not much sitting in kitten-sitting."